LIFE IN
ANCIENT EGYPT
Kate McArthur

Life in Ancient Egypt

Text: Kate McArthur
Editor: Rochelle Ransom
Design: Jennifer Warwick
Series design: James Lowe
Photo researcher: Corrina Tauschke
Production controllers: Renee Cusmano and Lisa Porter
Reprint; Siew Han Ong

Acknowledgements
The author and publisher would like to acknowledge permission to reproduce material from the following sources:
Alamy/imagebroker: pp. 1, 11, cover; Ancient Art & Architecture Collection Ltd/ J Stevens: p. 12; Corbis/Richard T. Nowitz: p. 21 (top); Getty Images: pp. 3, 8 (inset); Guy Holt © Cengage Learning Australia: p. 4; Photolibrary: pp. 21 (bottom), back cover; Photolibrary/The Bridgeman Art Library: pp. 8–9 (main); Photolibrary/PETER MENZEL/SPL: p. 5; Photolibrary/The Print Collector : p. 10; Photolibrary/Will & Deni McIntyre: p. 23 (inset); Virginia Gray © Cengage Learning Australia: pp. 6–7, 13–20, 22–23.

Every attempt has been made to trace and acknowledge copyright holders. Where the attempt has been unsuccessful, the publisher welcomes information that would redress the situation.

Fast Forward Independent Texts
Level 20

For product information and technology assistance,
in Australia call 1300 790 853;
in New Zealand call 0508 635 766

For permission to use material from this text or product,
please email **aust.permissions@cengage.com**

ISBN 978 0 17 017954 6
ISBN 978 0 17 017898 3 (set)

Cengage Learning Australia
Level 7, 80 Dorcas Street
South Melbourne, Victoria Australia 3205

Cengage Learning New Zealand
Unit 4B Rosedale Office Park
331 Rosedale Road, Albany, North Shore NZ 0632

For learning solutions, visit **cengage.com.au**

Printed in Australia by Ligare Pty Ltd
2 3 4 5 6 7 25 24 23 22

LIFE IN ANCIENT EGYPT

Kate McArthur

Contents

CHAPTER 1

THE BEGINNING OF ANCIENT EGYPT

Egypt is a very hot, dry country
where very little rain falls.
But there is a huge river
that runs through the middle of Egypt
called the Nile.
It is the longest river in the world.

The Nile River runs through Egypt and other parts of Africa.

The land next to the Nile River is very green. This is because every year, the river floods the land. When the water goes down, it leaves rich black soil which helps farmers to grow their crops.

About 5000 years ago,
people started to live along the Nile River.
Before then, people used to move from place to place
looking for plants to eat and animals to hunt.
But when they found the green land next to the Nile,
they stopped moving and stayed in the one place.

The people living by the river learned how to catch animals and farm them, so that they always had meat to eat. They also learned how to grow crops to eat. This was the beginning of ancient Egyptian **society**.

CHAPTER 2

Pharaohs and Pyramids

The pharaoh was the king of ancient Egypt.
The people believed
that a pharaoh was both a king and a god.
They believed that when the pharaoh died,
he went to live with the other gods.

This meant that the pharaoh had a lot of power
over the people of ancient Egypt.
The pharaoh made laws
that the common people had to follow.

Tutankhamen became a pharaoh in ancient Egypt in 1334 BC. His tomb was discovered more than 3200 years later.

ancient Egyptian farmers

The pharaoh ruled most of the land in ancient Egypt. The common people lived and worked on this land, planting crops and farming animals, but most of their produce went to the pharaoh. This was another reason why the pharaoh was so rich and powerful.

The people of ancient Egypt believed that if they looked after the pharaoh's body when he died, the pharaoh would live forever in the **afterlife**. So they wrapped up the pharaoh's body and turned it into a **mummy**.

A **pyramid** was built as a place to hold the pharaoh's body. It was often built during the pharaoh's lifetime.

*A mummy was placed in a special coffin called a **sarcophagus**.*

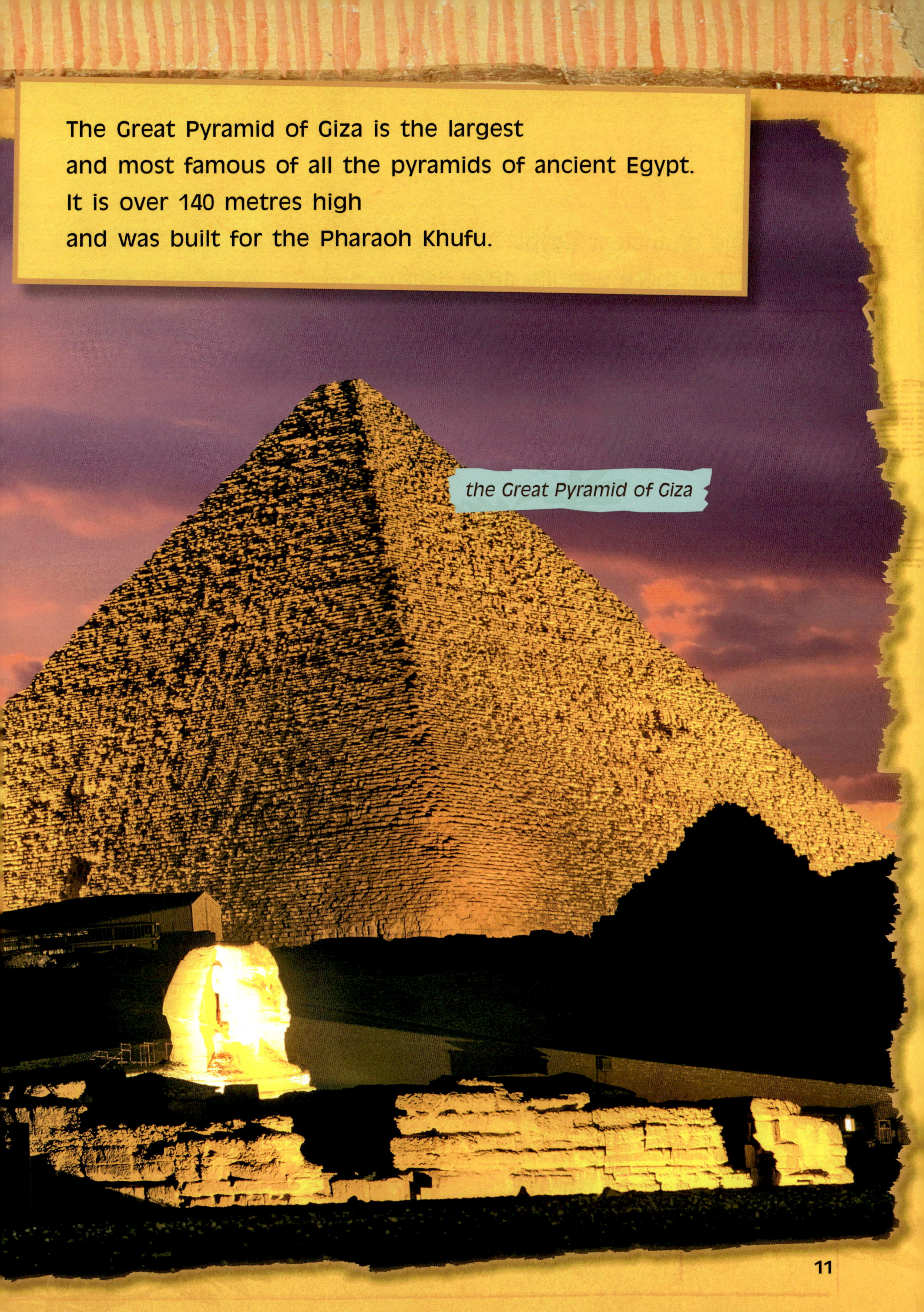

The Great Pyramid of Giza is the largest
and most famous of all the pyramids of ancient Egypt.
It is over 140 metres high
and was built for the Pharaoh Khufu.

the Great Pyramid of Giza

CHAPTER 3

RELIGION

The people of ancient Egypt believed that there was life after death for ordinary people. They thought that in the afterlife, dead people would need all the things that they had used in life.

Ra was the sun-god.

The family of the dead person would put food and clothes into the grave for the afterlife.

Anubis was a god who took dead people to the next world.

Osiris was a god who judged the dead.

The people of ancient Egypt also believed in many different gods.
They believed that Ra, the sun-god, was the king of all the gods.

CHAPTER 4

JOBS AND EDUCATION

There were many different groups of people in ancient Egypt.
Each group had a different level of power.

The pharaoh had the most power.
Priests were powerful
because they controlled the temples.
Nobles were from rich families,
and were born into a high position.

Peasants and workers formed the largest group
in ancient Egyptian society.
Servants and **slaves** were the least powerful group.

Not many children learned to read and write.
Only rich families sent their children to school,
while children in poor families got married
at a young age or had to go to work.

*A scribe was trained to read and write.
Only males were allowed to be scribes.*

pharaoh
priests, scribes and nobles
merchants
peasants and workers
servants and slaves

CHAPTER 5

Everyday Life

Family life was very important in ancient Egypt. Children were seen as a great gift from the gods. Rich families had slaves to help look after the children. In poor families, the mother looked after the children. If a man and a woman could not have a child, they would ask the gods for help.

a mud-brick house in ancient Egypt

The common people of ancient Egypt
lived in houses made from mud bricks.
There were no toilets,
so people put their waste in the Nile River
or threw it on the street.

The streets smelled very bad.
People spent a lot of time on the roofs of their houses,
because it was cooler and further away from the streets.

The rich people of ancient Egypt
lived in grand houses and had many slaves.
They had bath houses
where they could wash
and have the slaves pour jugs of water over them.
Poor people, however, had to wash in the river.

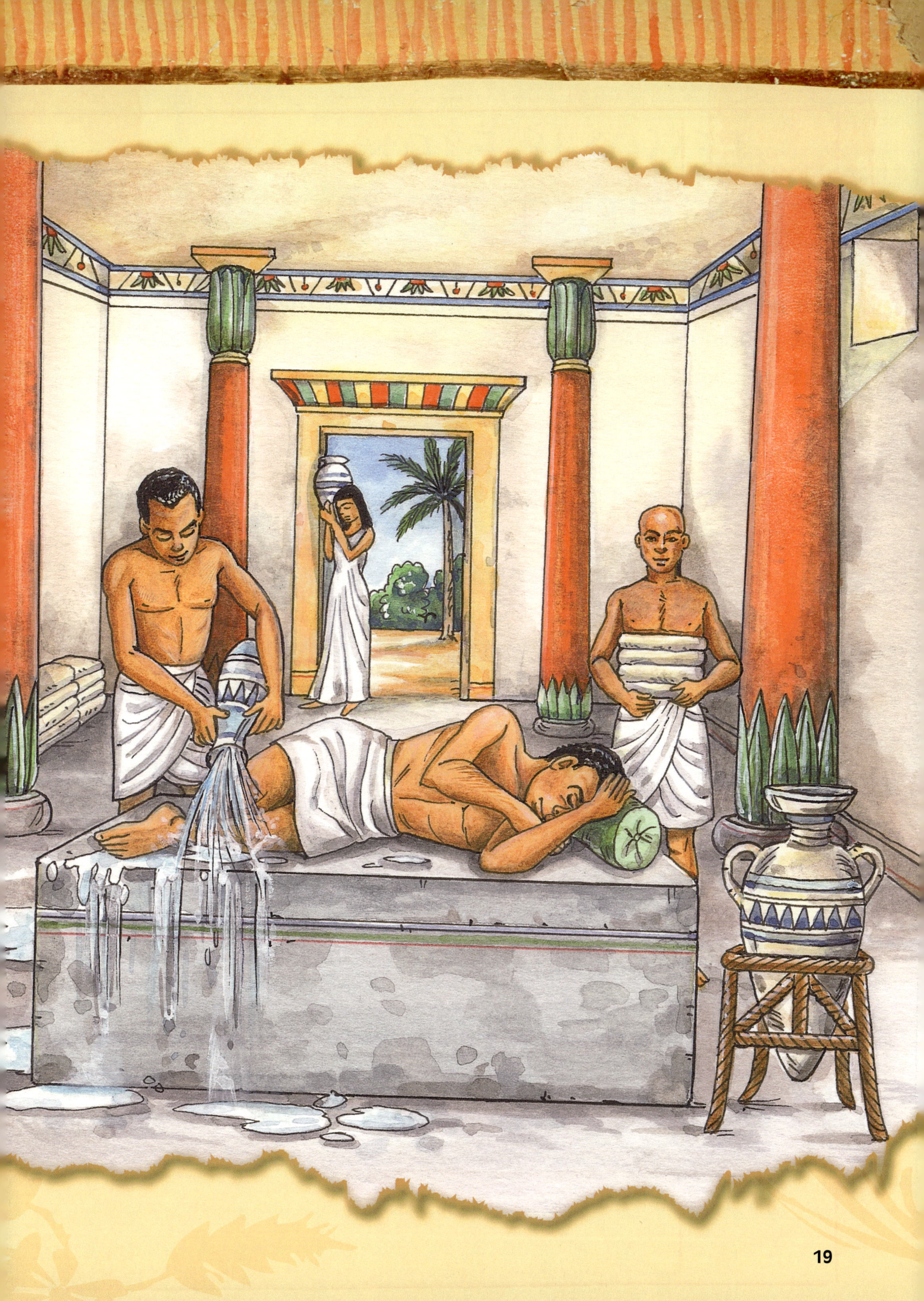

CHAPTER 6

LESSONS FROM ANCIENT EGYPT

The people of ancient Egypt invented lots of things that people still use today, such as boat sails, paper and calendars.

Ancient Egyptians invented a writing system called **hieroglyphics**.

They also made the world's first calendar.

The ancient Egyptians made significant advances in the development of religion, literature, art, science and mathematics.

Thousands of workers built the pyramids.

Without their knowledge
of complex mathematics,
architecture and engineering,
the ancient Egyptians would not
have been able
to build the pyramids.

Glossary

afterlife life after death

hieroglyphics a system of writing made up of different signs and symbols

mummy the body of a person or animal that has been preserved after death

pyramid a large structure built of stone, with a square base and four sloping sides which meet at a point

sarcophagus a stone coffin

slaves people who work for other people with little or no pay

society an extended social group of people, generally seen as members of a community

Index